My Blue World

Kimberly Knutsen

This is a work of fiction, and the views expressed herein are the sole responsibility of the author. Likewise, certain characters, places, and incidents are the product of the author's imagination, and any resemblance to actual persons, living or dead, or actual events or locales, is entirely coincidental.

Cover photo by Kimberly Knutsen

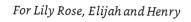

For Lily Rose, Elijah and Henry

1

"Oh girl, this boat is sinking, there's no sea left for me. And how the sky gets heavy, when you are underneath it…"
Macklemore, "Otherside"

Dear Macklemore,

I <3 you and my mom does too. We watched the "Thrift Shop" video and right away Mom says, "I want that coat." You are wearing a big fur coat like a lion. But I guess you know that because it is you. Ha.

I am me. Opal Jean. Yes, my mom gave me the ugliest name on the planet. But it is also a secret. Gene is my Dad's name. It is the kind of secret that makes you happy and sick at once.

My dad has been missing for eight years. He is in prison in Michigan. They took him when I was four. I don't know who "they" are.

"Quit fidgeting and do something," Mom said, so I am writing to you. We are on the plane, on the way to visit him for the first time since we moved to Portland. You are from Seattle. I read that. We're practically neighbors!

The plane smells like the inside of a plastic bucket. We are bouncing. My ears just popped. I hope we don't die.

When I think of my dad, I think of Juicy Fruit, Radiohead, and Built to Spill. Red Vines, too. He worked in Chicago. He came home on the weekends and brought me gum and licorice. He brought my brothers jerky.

I remember his leather jacket. It smelled like the cold sky.

It was always cold in Michigan and everything was blue. I remember standing in the dark in the driveway, the air full of ice crystals like we lived in a snow globe. My brothers built a snow cave with ice-blue walls. Giant icicles hung outside our kitchen window, shooting out rays of pink and blue.

Now we live in Portland, like a jungle but with traffic.

My mom has road rage.

I miss my cold blue world. It is where my dad lives.

His leather jacket. It's in our downstairs closet. My big brother tried it on last summer and it was WAY too small. It fit my dad. Obviously. I remember pressing my ear against his chest. Inside I could hear his heartbeat: bang, bang, bang. I used to laugh when he'd rub his whiskers against my cheek. Or throw me and my brothers onto the couch. He used to carry my middle brother around by his ankles, and David, who is weird, loved it. Dad would hold him upside down and parade around the living room, saying, "Look Ma, I found me a Pokémon." He tried it with me once, but I instantly screamed and cried. I'm a girl, Dad. Jeez!

He bought me a tutu and a tiara.

He let me eat ice cream for breakfast.

One day he brought home honey from Kenosha, a jar of golden light—like your song "Gold," Macklemore!

Oh, and more about me. I am twelve and I go to DaVinci, a performing arts middle school. I have curly blonde hair but I flatiron it. I am almost as tall as my mom. My teeth are crooked. Sometimes I want braces, but then I don't. In African drumming I play the djembe. You pronounce it "jim-bay." I play it so hard my hands hurt. It is my favorite class. Our teacher is Mr. D'Shawn, and if we are late we do pushups. No girl pushups, either.

I love you, Macklemore, because you are good. Not a good rapper—I mean you are—but a good person. Your songs are about things that matter, like drugs, and your friend's brother getting shot for his Nikes.

My dad did drugs. He shot and killed a man.

BANG, BANG, BANG. And then one day he was gone, only I didn't notice because I was just four. He never came home. He went to work in Chicago and did not return. There was a feeling in the house. Everything was dark, and the world slowed way down, like in a nightmare. But that was later, after we moved to Portland. Or was it? It's confusing. I knew my mom was scared and that scared me. Everyone was sad and I didn't know why, only that my dad did not come home, and then it had been a long time and I knew that he was not going to come home ever. I mean, how could he? We *left* home. We moved across the country. There was no home for him to go to.

2

In a hotel room in Chicago, high in the sky, planes whizzing past the windows. The world is futuristic. Skyscrapers and jet engines. We are stuck in the future. I want to go home. Back to the past. Back to my cold blue world.

My dad had a framed picture of airplanes on his bedroom wall. The colors were tangerine and silver and black. He said the style was Art Deco. I don't know what that is.

He dreamed of airplanes falling out of the sky. It was always the same dream, he said—a field, blue sky, the shadow of a jet. It wasn't scary. It was exciting.

Here is our disastrous trip so far—

We flew on the plane to Chicago and everyone was nervous. The plan was to continue on to Grand Rapids, meet Dad's mom and dad there, stay in a hotel, then drive to the prison in Ionia in the morning.

Riiiight.

I sat by Mom on the plane. She said, "Don't fidget." I wrote to you. It smelled like the inside of a bucket. David got trapped in the bathroom. He pushed the door instead of pulled. Matthew rescued him. "Genius was stuck," he said, grinning, looking cool in his gauges and black beanie.

"Were you in there this whole time?" Mom asked. David just smiled, pushed his glasses up on his nose.

4

The boys sat by strangers. Matthew talked to his stranger, a grandma in a glittery white cat sweatshirt, but he is eighteen and friendly to people who are not in his family. David hogged the snacks and played video games on his PS Vita, which is what he always does. He sat between a sleeping kid and a man in a suit who listened to The Bloody Beetroots on his computer. I know because I could see his screen. The heartbeat lines of his screen-saver pulsed to the beat of "Rocksteady." Why are we nervous? BECAUSE WE HAVE NOT SEEN OUR DAD IN SIX YEARS! Do you know how tall we've gotten? Matt is, like, grown up, with whiskers. Even David has hair on his upper lip—blonde hair, like a snow monkey.

Mom is the same height. Obviously.

I have a bra. Pink. Molded cups. I wore it once, but it was really uncomfortable.

We waited in the Chicago airport for, like, half a day. It was hot and stuffy. Our flight was delayed and delayed and then, just as we were about to board, it was canceled. The next flight to Grand Rapids was at six in the morning. "This is a nightmare," Mom said. We had only two days to visit Dad. Visiting hours started at eight a.m., and Ionia was almost an hour away from Grand Rapids. FYI: It's *prison*—you don't just drop in. Mom's cheeks got pink. She rattled the pills in her purse. She had to take a seat. When she was "grounded," we figured out the tickets, hauled our backpacks ten miles to a different part of the airport, then stood in line another forty minutes for hotel and food tickets.

When it was our turn, Mom sighed with relief. She chatted with the worker, an older lady with glasses shaped like alien eyes. The lady seemed kind of dumb because she couldn't figure out how to work the computer. I wanted David to go back there— he'd figure it out in two seconds flat.

"These kids haven't seen their dad in six years," Mom said.

"Why not?" The lady tapped her keyboard. Her glasses glowed blue in the light of the screen.

"He's incarcerated."

My ears perked up.

"Oh no, why?"

Big pause. *Mom, shut up. Mom, shut up.* The lady stopped tapping. The printer hummed. I could hear people in line behind us grumbling. "Well, um…drugs…" my mother said. "And then… murder…" Even when she's trying to be quiet my mom has the LOUDEST voice on the planet.

"Oh, MY."

Mom blinked, as if she'd found herself caught in a trap. She looked down at her hands on the counter. Matthew sighed, a disgusted look on his face, and walked away. David tugged on Mom's hand. "I feel really sick," he began. I was frozen. I wanted to disappear. I was phytoplankton in a sea of zooplankton. I would have happily been sucked into the belly of a whale, lived in its cage of ribs, listened to the steady BOOM of its heart—are whale hearts blubbery and blue?—and swished in its stomach with all the other fish and shrimp and partially digested seal parts.

The Chicago sky was white. It wasn't hot or cold—the air felt like nothing. But it was fresh and we could breathe again.

The future seemed brighter outside even though our luggage had continued on to Grand Rapids without us, and we didn't even have toothbrushes, only the little thumb-sized ones they gave us in our "courtesy bags" which contained—WTF?—a shoe polishing kit and the wateriest, worst smelling lotion you could imagine. PS: I was wearing flip-flops. Our shoes were halfway to Grand Rapids.

The shuttle dropped us at our hotel. MIDWESTERN MEAT MANUFACTURERS—MMM—WELCOM said the sign over the parking lot. Despite the missing E, a convention was going full force. Meat men in collared shirts swarmed the lobby. Their nametags read HELLO MY NAME IS… As Mom checked in, I watched them, sunglasses dangling from cords around their necks, phones clipped to their ears like fancy jewels. I made up names for their tags. HELLO MY NAME IS BOLOGNA. HELLO MY NAME IS CALF BRAINS. HELLO MY NAME IS TONGUE.

"M-M-M-men," I mumbled to myself.

Some looked like meat, pink and splotchy. Well, they were all meat, weren't they?

ROAST. BRAUNSCHWEIGER. NUGGETS—

I ran out of meats. We're practically vegetarian. No, that's not true. We're hamburger-centric. Mom makes four dinners and then she gets stuck and starts over. These are the dinners of my life: one quarter tacos, one quarter spaghetti, one quarter pizza, and one quarter this stir-fry chicken stuff that, for some reason, always tastes burned. It was my grandma who made roast.

In a blast of galactic ooze, I was homesick. Loneliness scooped out my guts and dumped them on the purple carpet even though my family was right there, leaning against the front desk: Mom, her dark hair falling out of its bun, mascara smudging her big eyes; Matthew with his buzz cut talking to the pretty clerk; and David in his hoody, zoned out to the dub step blasting on his headphones. Everyone was present, but the pets were at home— Sugar, Monkeygirl, Bob, Sparkle, El Diablo, Foxy and Caveman— and I felt like I might die.

Our hotel room was as high as the moon. I looked out the window at the lights of the city, big globs of glowworms under the purple twilight sky. My dad used to work there. He sold sausage casings. I don't know what those are. If he were free, he would be downstairs in the lobby with the other men, talking about meat. I wondered how many were dads. Most, I bet. I pictured their kids, happy to see them at the end of the week. The lights blurred into wobbly blobs. The moon swung on a thin green string. I felt sick—sick and excited in my belly—for tomorrow we would see him.

Dad.

Gene Jr.

Big Gene, his dad, would drive us to the prison in Ionia—if we ever made it to Grand Rapids.

I am Opal Jean and he is not dead and gone. He is alive. We used to visit him at his first prison in Muskegon before we moved away. I remember playing Uno with sticky cards and getting a cheeseburger—!—from the vending machine. He is alive. My cold blue world is real.

Our hotel room was cantaloupe and gold, with a big glass coffee table and a way better TV than at home. There was a living room, and two giant beds in the bedroom. After dinner, Matthew was restless. He went downstairs to smoke. He checked out the spa. But when he came back, he was still upset. "What is it?" Mom asked. "How can I help?"

"You can't." Matthew stared at his reflection in the window. He flexed his shoulder muscles. "I'm not trying to go crazy stuck in a room with my family." He looked at me and David sprawled on the couch watching *Ridiculousness*. "No offense," he said. I made a face. David laughed. A dog on the show had just barfed while "dancing" with another dog.

"Let me order a beer," Matt said, perking up.

"No." Mom didn't look up from her phone. She was playing "Words with Friends" with Grandma.

"C'mon."

"No."

"Mom, this is intense. We haven't seen Dad for, like, half our lives. And obviously I can't smoke like I need to when I'm stressed. Just let me—"

"No." Mom's voice was firm. "And smoking pot is going to ruin your life. You'll end up sitting on a couch when you're forty. You need to quit now."

"Oh my God, I'm not asking for a lecture. And *you're* sitting on a couch. What the hell does that even mean?"

"On a couch with a bong. Doing nothing. Eating cereal. Watching reality TV. Is that how you want to end up?"

I smiled to myself because that's what she does practically every night of the week—minus the bong, of course.

"MOM. I'm not trying to flip the fuck out. Can I please—"

She dropped her phone and sighed. "One," she warned. "That's it. And only if you promise to quit harassing me for the rest of the trip. I mean it, not one word. Don't talk to me again.

Not one word until we get home."

"Thanks, Mom. Love you."

"Love you, too."

And that's how my big brother gets his way—ALL THE TIME. He never gives up and nobody can outlast him in a fight.

I heard him order four Coronas when she was in the shower. But room service called back a few minutes later to get a credit card number (the tickets didn't work for alcohol) and he was busted. "Only one," Mom told the guy on the phone. Water dripped from her hair onto the black lilacs tattooed on her shoulder.

"Two," Matt said.

"One," she repeated, then hung up. "Four beers are like thirty dollars—are you kidding me? Plus, you're only eighteen. You shouldn't have any."

"It's European. A beer with dinner is normal. You said so yourself."

"But not four."

"Did I order four?" Matt's tone was rude.

"Uh, YEAH," Mom began, but then she shut up and I was glad. I HATE listening to them fight. My big brother is nice, like, two days a month. When he is loving and kind I always say, "It must be Matt's time of the month." This makes Mom smile. Her time of the month makes her UNloving and UNkind. She once threatened to flush our guinea pig down the toilet if we didn't clean its cage.

I haven't had a time of the month. Not yet.

We all slept in one room, like when we were little and curled up with Mom in the king-sized bed. Dad had his room in the basement. He said he didn't like getting kicked in the nuts when he was trying to sleep.

Macklemore, will you have kids? Never leave them. Take them on tour with you. Get them little noise-cancelling headphones. If I had a panda and I took it to shows, I would buy those so it wouldn't get scared.

The world can be loud and startling.

Our beds were crazy comfortable. Everyone agreed.
The toothpaste from the courtesy bags tasted like chalk.

3

Planes can fall from the sky. Your dad can do something UNBELIEVABLE. Like a magician whose trick is BAD, DARK, EVIL, WRONG. And my dad is none of those things. So how does the world make sense?

Other surprises: El Diablo, one of our cats, hopped through the torn kitchen screen with a mouse in his mouth. It escaped under the stove. Every night: MADNESS. The cat thundered up and down the stairs, the mouse shrieked, the dogs barked. One night it ran under David's door and hid behind my dollhouse. We tried to catch it but couldn't. Then one morning, Mom found it dead on the floor in the hall. She paid me to clean it up—$10! I used a hanger to push it onto the dustpan, then left it on the porch for Richard. Richard is Mom's friend. At first he put it in the garbage, but Mom was like, "hell no, are you kidding me, I'm freaking out, blah blah blah," so he took the gardening shovel and buried it down the street. Or so he said because he really buried it next to the recycling bin in *our* yard and Mom SMELLED IT five days later when the weather got hot. So that's the story of the mouse. It was huge. Oh, and it wasn't a mouse, it was a RAT. But Richard said, "don't tell your mom that," so I didn't.

A good surprise: I get In-Style magazine in the mail every month. It's addressed to me, Opal Jean Baker. I have no idea who bought it for me. It is just exciting. I love the hair and make-up and fashion. I've always loved those things. Next week at school is Spirit Week. Thursday is Childhood Obsession Day. I asked Mom what I loved when I was little. She said makeup and cleaning. It's true. I still do. When I was three, she found me drawing on my eyebrows with a Magic Marker. The secretary at our old school told her I was a movie star in a past life. Ha. I used to skip ballet class to stay with my babysitter and help her do housework.

I know you loved to draw when you were little, Macklemore, and you kept your room straight—just like me! Don't worry, I'm not a creeper. It's in your "Same Love" song. Have you ever been surprised, like really shocked? What if one day all the dogs on the planet started speaking Japanese? Or Sour Straws turned out to be poisonous? I once had a dream that an alien was on our skylight trying to get in.

I'm scared now, like a rat in a kitchen, like an alien on a rooftop, the toxic yellow sky blasting me with death rays.

What if...

What if, when I see my dad...

What if, when I see my dad...

I die...

because I am so sad?

Visiting day. We sat in a brown and orange restaurant in Grand Rapids. A pancake on a plate looked up at me: blueberry eyes, orange slice smile.

It was nearly eleven. I sat squished between my brothers. We'd been up since four in the morning. The restaurant smelled like the inside of a coffee pot. Ugh. Nobody could eat.

David typed the number 8008135 into the calculator on his phone: BOOBIES. Everyone laughed, even Dad's mom and dad, Big Gene and Marlene.

"Dude," Matt said, surprised because David is usually quiet around him. They are four years apart and Matt and I are six years apart—we are from different eons. There are a million baby pictures of Matt and he has *three* baby books. There are hardly any baby pictures of me and I have exactly zero books documenting my life. Well, that's not true. Last year I made my own. I glued in all my school pictures—I was a poodle with rabbit teeth in first grade—plus a picture of a panda, a pink cow, and all my family members including my cousin Goose, who is three and has dimples just like me.

David was a preemie. He weighed two pounds. Our guinea pig Sparkle weighs two pounds. My brother is fine now, but Mom still treats him like he's fragile. If she could shrink him down and carry him around in her purse, she would. She is always asking if he needs protein or water, like he's a science experiment that's going to blow if she doesn't watch closely. David is not allowed to drink soda because "he crashes," but Mom will buy Monsters for Matt, which are, like, deadly.

David has a box that Mom painted and dusted with glitter. Inside is a crucifix, doll-sized pajamas, and a diaper the size of my palm.

"His teacher told me he's the class clown, can you believe it?" she said now, setting down her water glass.

"Uh oh, watch out," Marlene chuckled. "Gene Jr. was the class clown, and boy was he a handful."

Awkward silence.

Tip #1: If your dad has killed someone, people might look at you funny. They might wonder what you are capable of. *You* might wonder what you are capable of. This is a very scary thought. Quit thinking it immediately. Do not slide under the booth and cry. Or do if that helps.

Marlene has a soft Southern accent. Her hair is silver and blonde. She is polite. Big Gene is manly like a truck. You don't mess with Big Gene. He takes care of business. For example, when our luggage was not in Grand Rapids this morning—when it was LOST—he told the worker he'd better find it ASAP or heads were going to roll.

I imagined heads like bowling balls rolling around the baggage carousel.

"You'll never see it again," he told Mom now, stabbing a forkful of steak and eggs.

Marlene agreed. "It was on one of those shows," she said. "Workers steal the suitcases, then sell everything inside."

HUH?!

I looked at David and he gave me a secret smile.

"What's so funny?" Matthew asked.

"We packed our sock monkeys—all fifteen of them."

"Why on earth," Mom said.

I shrugged.

"You guys still play with those?" Matt laughed. "Do you?" he asked David. "Dude, you're almost in high school."

David just smiled.

"They have names and we marked them off on a check-list," I explained. "Bilbo, Schmocko, Schmunks, Starbücks, Horn Bridgie..."

Matt looked at me like I was crazy.

I giggled. "I can't remember the rest because they're on the checklist that we packed. But what I want to know is who is going to buy them?"

"What are you talking about?" Matthew said.

"The people who steal the suitcases. Are they going to sell the sock monkeys? And who will buy them? Because they're all missing either their tails or," I took a sip of soda, "their limbs. Be-cause of the—"

"*Limbs*,'" David whispered in a Beavis and Butthead voice.

I laughed so hard I spit Sprite on the table.

"Digits," he added. "Heh heh." And then I couldn't stop. I kept picturing an airport worker holding up our chewed and slob-bered on sock monkeys, SELLING THEM TO RANDOM PEOPLE, and then I pictured the different monkeys—the one with its head bandaged in pink duct tape, the one wearing the underwear from my American Girl doll—and my cheeks got hot and I didn't know if I was laughing or crying, only that I couldn't stop.

Marlene smiled nervously.

"Jean," Mom scolded. "Get a hold of yourself."

"I hate to interrupt your little story," Matthew said, "but I really need a cigarette." He turned to Big Gene. "I'm trying to quit but it's not going to happen today. Do you think we could stop at a store or something?"

"No problem buddy." Big Gene nodded at his wife. "Your grandma smokes too."

"I do not." Marlene's voice was indignant.

Big Gene grunted.

"Well...only on special occasions."

Mom touched Marlene's arm. "I used to smoke."

"We've all smoked," Big Gene said. His voice sounded sad, and I was scared—I don't know why. We sat in silence. The carpet was brown with orange wedges. If I squinted they blurred into suns. After a minute, Big Gene raised his hand for the check. It was time to drive to Ionia.

4

Why We Are Happy David is the Class Clown

David is in the eighth grade now, but he didn't go to school for the entire seventh grade. He had anxiety, but we didn't know that then. We just knew he wouldn't go to school. We all rooted for him. "C'mon David, you can do it." Grandma would call every night to see if he'd gone. But he couldn't. He wouldn't get out of bed, or if he did he'd get right back in after brushing his teeth and refuse to leave. One morning Mom forced him into the car and made him get out at school. She drove away. He called half a second later, crying, and she turned right back around. "Never again," she told Grandma that night. "I'm not going to make him suffer. If he can't do it he can't do it. It's the seventh grade. The world isn't going to end."

So David did online school which meant he played video games during the day while Mom was at work, then battled with her at night when it was time to do the assignments. Mom would end up doing most of it, only she couldn't do the math or the grammar stuff because she'd skipped most of high school, so Grandma would have to drive in from Tualatin, and she would be mad and say dire things to David like "what are you going to do with your life?" and "do you want to work in a gas station?" (when she said this, he looked excited) and "how are you going to support a wife and kids?"

It was a disaster.

David went to April the counselor. She gave him directions to hang on his bedroom wall: HOW TO GO TO SCHOOL. WHAT TO DO IF YOU'RE ANXIOUS. WEP: WATER EXERCISE PROTEIN. But mostly he drew cartoons to send to Dad. He had a check-up and he was fine. He went to a fancy doctor to test his brain and he was normal. I could have told them that for free. Fact: David is sad because HIS DAD IS IN PRISON. But I guess there's no test for that.

My brother is skinny with black-framed glasses. I am taller, but he is meaner when we wrestle. He goes to school every day now. Grandma said he'd start liking a girl and that would make him go. Well, guess what? It's true. He likes Sage. She is in the seventh grade. Her hair is dyed blue, green and yellow. Her mom is always late and so is ours, so they hold hands while they wait for their rides after school. Don't tell anyone.

5

The prison looked like a haunted castle. It sat on a hill surrounded by nothing. Behind us were woods—deep, dark woods. Had we walked into or out of a fairytale? I had no idea. I looked at my brothers. Matthew had no expression. David seemed excited.

The officer at the front desk told us we would have to wait for count to end—count is when they count the inmates, duh—so we decided to walk around town. We looked at buildings. I know every kid on the planet has walked around a strange town looking at buildings with their grandparents. WOW! There is nothing so boring. We stared at a giant bell. "In France, instead of the Easter Bunny they have a bell," Mom said. No one answered. David rang the bell. "Run," Matthew joked.

The sky was dark. The air was hot and still. "Tornado weather," someone said. A flash of memory: I am eating my dinner of brats and tots in the babysitter's basement because the sirens have just gone off. I keep looking at the washer and dryer. I really hope we'll get to do laundry after we eat.

At 12:55 we walked back up the steep hill. The light had changed. The sky was bright—it hurt my eyes—and the air smelled like the bottom of a swimming pool. I waited for the tornado to come, to suck us into the heavy sky. I felt green and barely able to breathe. I thought of the lyrics from one of my dad's favorite songs. WHY SO GREEN AND LONELY? I put it on my T-shirt in printmaking over a picture of a Kewpie doll in a bathing cap. Lori Sumac, who is stupid, walked by and said, "What is THAT?" Like

I'd done something weird.

"If you want weird—" I wanted to say.

My dad killed the man on Halloween. He was supposed to take us trick or treating, but he never did. Obviously. I was a bee that year. Who cares? I was always a bee back then. And I still love Halloween. I'm not going to let ANYONE ruin it. David gets tired of trick or treating and gives up. He'd rather play video games. He waits until I bring home my candy, then eats that.

I am the only one in my family who tries.

We walked past the yard. It looked like a playground, but there were no swings or monkey bars. Men in blue outfits walked around a track. *Criminals*, I thought although they looked normal. The yard was surrounded by a high fence with loops of wire on top. "Razor wire," David said. There was a tower at one end, but instead of a princess it held a guard with a rifle. This wasn't a fairy tale, it was one of David's video games with exploding body parts and machine guns. It was *Cops* on TV. I wanted to go home.

"It doesn't get easier," Marlene said.

I looked at Mom. She didn't answer.

At the door we handed our phones to Marlene. A sign on the building read NO PURSES, CELL PHONES, OR CAMERAS ALLOWED IN THE FACILITY. Big Gene said they'd be back for us at 4:00—he and Marlene would visit later that night. "Here you go, sir." He handed David a twenty-dollar bill. "Get some quarters. Buy everyone snacks."

"You can have your picture taken too," Marlene added.

Mom hesitated. "Maybe 3:30," she began. "The kids... It's awfully hard—"

"I agree. 3:30 it is. And then we'll go back and go swimming. How does that sound?"

The boys nodded.

"Yay," I said in a sickly voice.

Marlene hugged me. I closed my eyes and let her. She smelled like lemon perfume and hairspray. I wanted to go with her and Big Gene to look at antiques. Yes, BORING. But also not scary. Grandmas are SAFE. They don't go off and kill people for

KIMBERLY KNUTSEN

NO REASON AT ALL.

6

In the hotel room, part girl part fish. Later that night. My fingertips are white and shriveled. I am drinking 7-up. My hair smells like pool water and I am floating, floating—

Dear Macklemore,

It wasn't like I thought it would be.

My dad has shrunk and I have grown bigger—

I can't even—

(teardrops)

Have you ever visited someone in prison? If not, here's how it goes. "Pee before you go in," Mom would tell you, but we didn't. Then: wait. We waited and waited until finally it was our turn. Nobody could breathe. David jingled the baggy full of quarters. The guard swiped the backs of our hands with invisible ink. David thought that was cool. It was cool because in the next room we had to stick our hands under a purple light and there it was—the swirl of invisible ink.

The lady officer was nice. "Hey little mama," she said. "Show me your feet."

You have to show the bottoms of your feet—no socks, no shoes—and the INSIDE OF YOUR MOUTH LIKE YOU ARE AT THE DENTIST. Next we stood with our arms out while the lady patted down me and my mom and a male officer patted down my brothers. Just like on *Cops* only nobody was drunk and nobody tried to run.

When it was Matthew's turn I was nervous. I remembered

Mom telling him to search the pockets of his cargo shorts and make sure there was no weed in them, "not a seed, not a stem." But what if there was a seed or a stem? Would they take my brother too? And then I was REALLY MAD—at my brother for smoking pot, and at them, whoever they were, for taking away the one person I cared about on the planet.

I tried to be brave but I wasn't. My heart crashed like a broken washing machine, and my arms felt funny, full of bubbles and suds. I looked at Mom. She made her eyes big like OMG, I'm freaking out, and then I felt better. The boys were quiet.

We followed the guard into another room and there he was —Dad. I was confused. I wasn't ready. I am Opal Jean, I am Opal Jean, and there he was, sitting on a bench in normal clothes, waiting for us. It didn't feel real. It was like a dream, like the ones where he shows up and just stands there smiling, as out of place as if he'd suddenly appeared on the TV screen in the middle of Bikini Bottom. Long blonde ponytail, tattoos, whiskers. "Here's my people," he said. He jumped up to hug us, first David, then Matthew, and then it was my turn.

Gene Jr.

Dad.

I didn't feel anything. I was confused. I'd thought he would be in *another* room, and that we would walk to that other room and wait some more, like we'd been waiting for half the day, or for the past week, or for most of our lives if you wanted the truth.

Tip #2: Be ready.

Tip #3: Know that you can *never* be ready. You will not be ready when your dad leaves. He'll disappear in an explosion of light. The magician will wave his wand and—poof!—your dad is gone. Parts of him will remain: his shoes in a box in the garage; his leather jacket, which fits no one, hanging in the downstairs closet. One day your mom will think it's a good idea to make a pillow out of his pink dress shirt, the one he's wearing in the pictures of your first dance recital. And you will know, as well as you know your toes, that this pink pillow, the one the big dog Bob likes to carry around and lick, is the end—the very end—of Dad.

And then he'll reappear!

In the visiting room, Dad hugged me for a long time. I felt nothing. His chest was warm against my cheek and when I breathed in I knew it was him, his smell like a lost teddy bear I'd forgotten that I'd loved, and then I felt sad and it scared me. "There are so many rooms," I said, "and I thought there would be another—"

"A what?"

"—and that we would wait."

"What?"

"Wait."

"Wait? For what?"

I didn't answer. It was like that: electricity zapping around the room, everybody stunned.

Dad looked at Mom who shrugged. He held my face in his hands. "Look at you. You look so pretty, you look so grown up."

I ducked away. "Our luggage is lost, probably stolen. We've been wearing these clothes for days and when we bought toothpaste we forgot to buy deodorant—so we all stink." I wanted to sound hard but I didn't. My voice was high and frantic. "And Mom isn't even wearing underwear," I added, "because—"

"That's enough," Mom said, an amused look on her face.

The vending machines had weird things like tuna salad and sausage French toast. I didn't eat. I didn't want to die of food poisoning. Dad and the boys snacked. Mom got a Diet Coke. The room was small and hot with big fans spinning in the corners. I watched one until I was dizzy, unable to talk or move.

The room was crowded. Most of the inmates wore blue prison outfits with orange stripes on the legs and white numbers on the shoulders. My dad has a number—573546. It won't change. It will stay with him for life.

Did I tell you my dad is serving a life sentence?

When we were little we'd ask Mom, "When will Dad get out? Will it be when we're old? Like in high school?"

She always said that Dad would be free when God decided

he should be free because it was God who ran the universe and not the Michigan Department of Corrections.

"So...he'll get out when?"

Last year I looked it up on the internet. I learned that there are two kinds of life sentences: *life as in twenty years*, like what the man who cooked and ate his wife got, and *life without the possibility of parole*, as in *never* and *forever*, which is what my dad got.

(And isn't it weird that never and forever are the exact same thing?)

I presented the information to Mom because I wanted to be wrong. She said that *everyone* is serving a life sentence and that dad is freer on the inside than he ever was addicted to drugs on the outside, and that if he hadn't gone to prison he would be dead by now of an overdose.

"So it's a good thing?" I cried. "Death or prison? Those are the choices?" We were making cookies. I dumped the flour into the batter. A white cloud exploded in my face. I quit thinking.

I still don't think about it.

Certain things are *unthinkable.*

Tip #4: KNOW THIS.

Back to the visit. Some inmates wore normal clothes. You could tell them from the regular men because their jeans were dark-washed and stiff. Most of the visitors were ladies and kids. One man had four little girls lined up beside him, the youngest in braids decorated with colorful plastic barrettes. His wife or girl-friend wore a tight purple dress. I wondered how she got away with it. Before we packed, Mom said, "not too tight, not too baggy; Matt, you can't sag your pants, no demonic pictures on your shirts, no you cannot wear the MOSH MOTHERFUCKER T-shirt; no hoodies, sorry Ben, I don't make the rules; no cleavage—that's for me to remember, no, no, no."

Wearing the correct clothing, we sat by the guard booth. It looked like a DJ booth, but the guard was definitely *not* bopping around in a giant mouse head. He was big with a shaved head, and he looked mean. The rule: stay seated in your own plastic seat.

The seats were bolted to the floor, so we took turns sitting next to Dad. David was first. Like the lady in the tight purple dress —like everyone in the room—he seemed happy. He told stories and laughed and held Dad's hand even though he is fourteen. His jeans were stained with blueberry syrup, and his T-shirt said S'UP DAWG over a picture of a hamburger greeting a hot dog. "This is what he needs," Mom said. "If David could spend the summers with you, his life would be perfect."

"Is that true?" Dad asked.

David nodded.

Dad looked thoughtful. "Like a 'Take Your Kid to Prison' day—"

"Or like *Scared Straight*," Matt said. "Those kids are punks."

"Or the programs that give you a puppy," David added. "We read about it in school. You train them to be helper dogs, and they're mostly Labs like Bob."

"I would love a puppy like Bob." Dad looked at me. "Hey Opal, how is old Bob? Does he still like to swim in the kiddy pool?"

I shook my head. Sadness was choking me. I knew if I opened my mouth to speak, I would collapse inward like a black hole and the entire universe would follow.

"He's old," Mom said. "He dribbles."

David got up to buy water. He was obsessed with the vending machines. Matthew moved to sit by Dad. While they discussed the "spiritual awakening" Matt had after wrecking his car, I stared at Mom's newest tattoo. It was a portrait of Janis, the cat before we were born. Janis stared at me from Mom's upper arm, a tiny smile on her face. She was inked mostly in black and gray, but the tips of her fur were turquoise—for luck, Mom said. Her eyes were green.

I hated Janis. Not because I actually did—I never knew the stupid cat—but because I wanted to hate something, and a dead cat is an easy target. A banner curved beneath her chin whiskers. JANIS—as if she had been a beauty queen, the prettiest kitty in town.

Where was Janis now?

(dead)

Where were we when Janis prowled the earth, catching mice in Mom's college apartment, dropping them on her futon, bloody gifts of whiskers and guts and fur?

(not yet alive)

And where did the souls of the dead mice go?

(I had no idea)

Everyone disappears.

No one is here at the same time.

I felt sick.

"What about boxing?" Dad asked Matthew. Matt is a good boxer—undefeated. At his last match, the ring doctor told Mom that if he trained seriously, he could one day be in the Olympics. We had a boxing room in our house in Michigan. There was a punching bag and a poster of Muhammad Ali. Dad boxed too.

"It's going OK," Matt said. "I'm working on my cardio. The smoking, you know—"

"Oh, I know. They made us quit. All tobacco products banned." Dad paused, and when he spoke again his voice was stern. "You need to stop smoking."

Matthew was quiet. I guess there wasn't much to say about that—or about boxing. His last match was a year ago. He hasn't been to the gym in a long time. I know because Mom asks him about it and he gets mad.

"I know you'll quit—when it's time." Dad rested his hand on Matthew's shoulder. Matt hung his head and started to cry. I froze. Everyone was quiet. "It's OK, buddy." Dad's voice was low. "I don't blame you. I fucked up. And I am so, so sorry."

Matt lifted his head and wiped his nose on his sleeve. He started to say something but broke into sobs again. Mom touched his knee. David handed him the bottle of water.

My family looked small and far away. They looked like cartoon characters. Mom with her messy knot of hair and big, sad eyes. Matthew with his Buddha necklace and lotus flower tattoo.

David looked worried. He pushed his glasses up on his nose and stared at his big feet. He hates it when any of us are upset—it scares him.

I thought *what a mess*.

Dad wore normal clothes. He had ordered them especially for our visit. The jeans were OK, but the shirt—a summery shirt like what a dad might wear to a church picnic—was way too big. Dad is skinny and not too tall, and the "short" sleeves went all the way down to his elbows.

It was the shirt that broke my heart.

He kept saying how sorry he was, how his addiction had destroyed everything—no, *he* had destroyed everything, and if he could change the past, if he could go back in time... Dad shifted in his seat, no longer cheerful but upset. "If I could die and take away all the pain I've caused you guys, all the pain I've caused *everyone*, I would do it in an instant—"

"You don't have to die," David cried.

"That's upsetting," Mom said.

"But it's true. If I could go and take all the pain I've caused with me, if I could set everyone free—"

"You're not Jesus," Mom said.

"—if I could set everyone free..." Dad's face crumpled. When he rubbed his jaw his hand shook.

I closed my eyes.

"Changing the subject..." Matt blew his nose on a napkin. He stuffed a Honey Bun in his mouth. Dad settled back in his seat. The twister had not touched down. "It's your turn," Mom said. I shook my head.

"Sit by Dad." Matt gave me a poke. "He's going to feel like you don't—"

"It's OK." Dad touched Matt's arm. "Let her be. Opal will move when she's damn good and ready." He smiled. "Right?"

I nodded.

Mom switched seats with Matt and the talk turned to boring things: *Mad Men* and books and the art show in Ann Arbor that had sold Dad's paintings.

I watched my dad. As he spoke, he seemed to grow smaller, his eyes larger and more afraid. His voice became creaky. It was as if he were aging by the second. I thought of the YouTube video we'd seen in science, the one of the dead baby pig that turned from a pig to a puddle to a pile of maggots in less than six minutes. And then: nothing.

I thought *his six minutes are almost up.*

Did prison do that to a person? Did time speed up when all you had was time?

Dad—my dad, Gene Jr.—would one day be gone. And I was alive, not even close to dead. I was beginning as he was coming to an end. And the dad I'd known when I was small—bringer of Red Vines, thrower of kids onto the couch—had disappeared a long time ago.

I didn't want to know what I knew, but I knew that I was right.

I felt myself growing larger. (I wanted to stop, I wanted to be small.) My octopus head wobbled. My squid legs tangled around the chair. It was so hot. Everyone was so happy, so LOUD. Why wasn't there any air conditioning? And why was the room shrinking? I felt trapped in a nightmare and I had to wake up. WAKE UP.

"I want to go," I said, squeezing my eyes shut tight. Nobody heard. "Let's get OUT OF HERE," I cried. Panic jolted my body. My head was sinking. I knew I was going to die. Mom looked up. I burst into tears. She reached out and pulled me close and I stayed there, caught in the circle of her arms, until I could breathe again.

When we got up to go, I couldn't look at Dad.

$$7$$

**I am drinking pool water. My hair smells like 7-
Up and I am sinking, sinking—**

So that was the visit, Macklemore.
It was not good.
I was not happy.
I was GLAD when it was time to go and we could run outside into the heavy sky where Big Gene and Marlene waited. I'd
never been so happy to leave a place in my life. I was happy to
leave my dad sitting alone in prison where he will be for THE
REST OF HIS LIFE. That is the kind of girl I am: Opal Jean, glad to
go, glad to be free, glad to be me—mean Opal Jean.

PS: Tomorrow we go back. I hope I do better.

PPS: Did you ever do anything bad when you did drugs—besides
doing drugs? In the video for "Otherside," you overdose in the
bathtub. My mom likes that part not because you die, but because you are cute and in the bath so, you know…not dressed. But
the guy in the video isn't you, obviously. And it wasn't my dad
who killed the man on Halloween, not the dad I knew. It was a
story in the paper, a story on the TV news, a transcript on the
internet, but it was never really my dad, not the dad I knew.

After the visit, we partied like rock stars.
Why? Because we were free. Because all the feelings to feel

had been felt, and now we would only feel good.

Matthew smoked outside the car before we got in to drive back to Grand Rapids. "You *have* to let me get a beer tonight," he told Mom.

"I'm with Matt," Big Gene said, unlocking the doors. "Grandma and I will have a nice stiff scotch after our visit."

"We will not," Marlene scolded.

Mom got an iced latte. Big Gene stopped at a coffee place that was like a Starbucks but not. The teenage girl who helped us wore a pink visor and a pin that said *You Are Loved.* "You're adorable," she said when she took my order. When she handed me my hot chocolate there was a Gummi Bear plopped on top of the whipped cream. "Isn't that cute," Marlene said. David asked if he could have it and I said no way.

Mom pulled the paper off her straw. "Gene looks good," she said, "but—" She stopped talking. Her eyes got shiny. I leaned my body against hers, and she stumbled backward, then laughed, embarrassed.

"It wasn't the plan," Big Gene said, dumping a handful of change in the tip jar.

Back in the car, we sat in the middle backseat. The boys were in the back. There are two backseats in Big Gene's car, and everyone can control their own air conditioning. I turned ours on full blast. The car was so big, the ride so smooth and comfortable, it was as if we were floating down the highway, away from Ionia, away from the prison and the yard and the razor wire and my dad. "Don't mind the leopard," Marlene said. I looked down at the floor beside my feet. Big Gene and Marlene had bought a black metal leopard "for the fireplace." It had dark spots but no tail. Don't leopards have tails? I'm pretty sure they do. "There's no tail," I started to say, but I was almost asleep, and the words dissolved into my dream.

Back at the hotel, David and I swam. In the deserted pool next to the empty fitness room: GIANT ASTEROID EXPLOSIONS, STAR-FISH BATTLES TO THE DEATH, SOCK MONKEY OLYMPICS. Before swimming, we stopped at Target where Big Gene and Marlene bought us swimming suits and goggles. We also got sweatpants and T-shirts, underwear and deodorant, and eyeliner for Mom. Our luggage was still lost.

We stayed in the pool for hours, until we were blue through and through.

8

**In a purple world. The sky is tilted. Trees crack.
The grass warps beneath my feet.**

Mom and the boys crashed early. I curled up on the cot near the door and watched three episodes of *Pretty Little Liars* on Mom's phone. By the time season one ended, and I still didn't know who A was, it was a little after nine.

The mini-fridge hummed. Someone coughed in the hallway. My hair reeked of chlorine. It was sticky and my curls were wild, twisting from my head like vines. I wore my mom's tie-dyed T-shirt. I looked like a hippy.

I couldn't sleep. After the excitement of my favorite show, the sadness was back. It sat like a chimp on my chest, heavy and dumb. *I have a problem*, I thought, and the thought surprised me because it had always seemed that only other people—like the girls on *Teen Mom 3*—had problems that were real and not like why can't I get my cartilage pierced?

I pulled the jungly bedspread up to my ears. The wind bounced against the windows. Shadows shivered on the walls. I missed the sounds of home, the dogs snoring and kicking in their dreams, the click of Sparkle's water bottle, the rustle and thump as he hopped around his cage. I couldn't sleep because I didn't want to wake up. Tomorrow was the final visit: the stuffy room, the fans whirring like the fear in my chest, my shrinking dad.

I couldn't do it.

I didn't want this.

My life felt like the skinny jeans I made Mom buy that were way too small, and she told me so, she said "you need a 12," but I didn't listen, and when I wore them to school I couldn't breathe, I could barely sit, and my stomach hurt by the end of the day.

My life was too tight. I needed wiggle room. I needed room to breathe.

I thought of my health teacher Mrs. Bronson. One afternoon she said, "If you have a problem, fix it. We are not pretty paper dolls. We have agency. We can act upon our environments. Don't let your environment act upon you." This was the beginning of the "don't do drugs" talk which somehow turned into the "don't get date-raped" talk, and while I knew I would NEVER do drugs, and I didn't plan on dating until I was at least sixteen, her words stuck with me. I began to change the things I didn't like. There was this one piece of hair that always flipped the wrong way so I cut it off at the root. (*Big mistake*, Mom said.) I didn't like David eating all the chips so I started to hide them in the bathroom cupboard where I knew he would never look. (*Are these really Doritos next to the TOILET BRUSH*? Mom shouted.)

I thought of the bear. When I was in first grade, we spent hours gluing small brown pieces of construction paper onto a cutout of a bear. "It's a mosaic," the teacher said. HAPPY FATHER'S DAY! the parent helper wrote on the back. I signed my name: OPAL JEAN in big, crooked letters. Mom sent the card to Dad. Every time he called I would ask, "Did you get my bear?" But he never did. Months later it came back in the mail with a form from the prison. NO GLUED ITEMS ACCEPTED. When I asked Mom why, she said that, according to the prison, someone could have glued drugs to the back of the small brown pieces of paper. I cried then. That someone was me. I had done something bad.

In Portland, no one knows I have a dad. He is invisible like the disappearing ink. Sometimes he appears as a voice on the phone or a signature on a card: Love, Your Dad.

Last winter I played with a girl named Mercy after school, then stayed for dinner. She had a grandma who was wrinkled like a shrunken apple head doll and who rolled through the living room on a walker that had TENNIS BALLS on the bottom. The grandma disappeared into the kitchen then, minutes later, rolled back into the living room. All night she circled and smiled and asked me, "Who are you, darling?" I said Opal about sixteen times.

For dinner we had rice and peas and green beans too. Mercy's mom, with her one-sided haircut and sweater cape, asked did I want soy milk or water. I said neither because I wasn't thirsty and soy milk is disgusting (I didn't say the last part). She set down her fork. "We know your mom is a teacher, Opal, but what does your daddy do?"

I froze. My face got hot and I was sure everyone at the table —Mercy and her mom and her dad and the shrunken apple head grandma—knew the truth. Tears filled my eyes but I pretended I was fine. "I don't know."

"You don't know?"

"I mean… I'm not sure." My voice was a whisper. I focused on my peas. I ate every single one even though I HATE PEAS.

After dinner, Mom came to pick me up. We stood in the living room. The grown-ups talked. I zoned out until Mercy's mom said, "We asked Opal what her daddy does but she didn't know." She laughed then, sticky and sweet, and I hated her—and Mercy— and Mercy's dad, breathing on the couch like a big, dumb dog.

"He's a writer," Mom said.

"I love writers," said the grandma. "I once had a boyfriend who was a writer—"

"Oh, Mom, you did not." Mercy's mom looked annoyed.
In the car Mom told me that my business was my own, and I didn't have to share it with anyone. "Say your dad lives in Michigan and be done with it," she said, "not that there's anything wrong with where he is."

"Kind of," I said.

"What?"

"There kind of is…something wrong."

She looked confused, then picked up my hand. "You didn't

do anything wrong. You're not in prison. Do you feel like you're bad?"

"Yes, I do." I looked at the floor. "Sometimes."

She didn't answer. She looked sad. Then I felt doubly bad for disappointing my mom, for not being happy.

Tip #5: EAT DINNER AT YOUR OWN HOME.

Now, sitting in the hotel room in Grand Rapids, I was done. I was tired of feeling like a particle in a cartoon crazy world. Mom was right. Why should I feel bad when I didn't do anything wrong? Mrs. Bronson said *we have agency*. That means you can choose NOT to do drugs. Wrapped in the thin bedspread, shivering in the air conditioning, I finally got it. I don't have a dad. I, Opal Jean Baker, am fatherless. Invisible ink is just that: invisible. My cold blue world was a mirage. It was a sad, blue planet spinning in the sky. It was a seed that would never grow, a dream that would always end. It was a wilted blue flower, smashed in a memory book, crumbling at the edges, fading to the color of a biscuit.

I closed the book.

My problem was Gene Jr.—and it was a problem I could fix.

9

Dear Macklemore,

Here is the ending to my story. It isn't good or bad—it just is.

Before going to bed, I emailed my dad.

First I looked at Words with Friends on Mom's phone. Grandma had played SQUINTY for 80 points. I added LAP for 5 points. I knew Mom would be mad. I could hear her already: "don't do that, Grandma is a fierce competitor, every move counts, I can't afford your measly five points."

Lightning flashed. My hand turned white. I logged onto the internet, then went to J-Pay, the site you use to email a prisoner. They make you PAY to send an email. I guessed Mom's password on the first try: monkeygirl1. Her passwords are either monkeygirl, monkeygirl1, or BIGmonkeygirl. We've been hacking into her accounts for years. She may think she blocked Matt's phone after 11:00 p.m. on weeknights when he was in high school, but she never did—not for long.

I wrote without thinking and I wrote until I felt nothing, and when I was done and I had clicked SEND, I felt strange in a good way, like a bubble drifting in the sky, and everything, the whole liquid universe, was oxygen and rainbows and light.

I lay on the cot, floating in my mind. I heard the elevators groan and the same person—or maybe it was a different person—cough.

And then the sirens went off.

I sat up in the dark, unsure if I was dreaming, and when I knew I wasn't, when the sirens kept blaring and I'd pinched my thigh and it hurt, I got up to wake my family.

"Is it someone's phone?" Mom asked, shrinking like a bat from the light I'd clicked on.

"It's the tornado sirens. They're coming from outside."

"They're not very loud." She looked doubtful.

"Can you hear them?" I said. "Because I can. I'm listening right now. I think they mean we need to move."

She rolled over and pulled on her sweatpants. "Do we go in the bathroom, in the bathtub—" The phone on the night table between the beds rang. We stared at it. Mom picked it up. She listened, then hung up. Her eyes were wide. "We have to go down to the lobby. This is, like, a big deal. Wake up your brothers and grab your phone. And maybe we should brush our teeth first."

"Are you kidding? Did they say to go now? Or did they say to go but first brush your teeth?"

"You're so strict." Mom smiled. "Now, where the hell is my bra?"

The boys got up and stumbled into the hallway. Matt pushed the elevator button. "No elevators," Mom said, twisting her hair into a knot. "We need to take the stairs."

"Why?" Matt pushed the button again. "This isn't 9/11. You don't take elevators when there's a *fire*—"

"Are you really going to argue with me?"

"Quit arguing with me. Why are you so rude?"

"I am not—" Mom quit talking. Her face was hard. It was the look she got when Matt was a jerk. It made me mad. "Be nice to Mom," I said. My voice was loud but I kept my eyes down.

"What do you mean 'be nice to Mom'?" David kicked at the carpet, grouchy in his Scooby Doo pajama bottoms. "Why?"

"Because she is ALL WE HAVE." Am I the only one in my family who GETS IT?

Matt laughed. "Look at you, all badass and shit."

"Shut. The. Hell. Up." I was scared as soon as the words were out of my mouth.

Matt lunged as if he were about to head butt me. I screamed and ducked. David laughed.

"You idiots stay here and fight," Mom said. "I'm going downstairs."

We waited in the place where they serve orange juice and Honey Bunches of Oats in the mornings. The chairs were covered with sucking purple flowers, and everything looked and smelled brand new. There was a toaster oven with bagels stacked beside it. It was bulky and old fashioned. Why not just use a toaster? David had a Queasy Bake Oven. He made some sort of brown slime once, but then the pan got stuck inside and we couldn't get it out. If I had a toaster oven, I would use it to warm sick pets.

There were about thirty guests in the lobby. That was what the hotel workers called us: "guests." As if it were a party, a big pajama and sweatpants party. Babies slept on laps, and a lot of the men, including Big Gene, went to work on their laptops and cell phones as if it were a normal day and not night. We squished onto a couch in the corner. I could smell my big brother's deodorant, and I closed my eyes and leaned against him, glad he wasn't mad. Big Gene and Marlene sat at a table beside us.

A girl in a navy vest and black rubber-soled shoes, like the ones Matt wears to his dishwashing job, told us that a tornado had touched down nearby, and that another one, a bigger one, was expected to hit in thirty minutes.

ZOMG. Did we only have thirty minutes to live?

It didn't seem real. It was as if the worker had announced that at 9:41 we would all be eaten by zombies. I tried to feel scared. I felt nothing.

A guest spoke up. "Hit *us*, like this hotel?" The man had a teddy bear belly. Mom would call his physique a "full Pooh." He wore running shorts that were WAY too short.

"Well," the girl said, "um... I certainly hope not." She looked at her partner, a boy in a navy windbreaker. He nodded but said nothing. "We're taking every precaution."

"I'm sure you are." The man smiled. "But when one books a room, one doesn't really expect to spend the night in the lobby, now do they?"

"Sir?"

"We paid good money for these rooms, rooms we can't occupy because someone had the idiocy to build a hotel in the middle of a tornado zone—"

"Actually," the boy cut in, "there's no such thing as a tornado *zone*—"

"Don't argue with me. I want to know who's going to fix this."

"Well." The girl laughed once, her eyes wild, then turned and walked away.

"Riiigghhht." The man's voice was sour, but his face was bright, as if he were having the time of his life. His wife or mom, a skinny lady in a knobby peach sweater, grabbed his arm and whispered in his ear. "I will not pipe down," he said in a loud voice.

Somebody laughed. I looked at Mom. "He's about thirty seconds from getting himself locked outside in the storm," she whispered.

"Or getting a good kick in the can," Big Gene said.

Marlene smiled.

I bit my lip. What if the man was right to be upset? Should we be scared? I touched Mom's sweatpants. She reached down and patted my hand but kept playing Candy Crush on her phone.

They gave us party favors: bottles of water and blue Nutri-Grain bars. We also got authentic military glow sticks, which sucked because we weren't allowed to open them unless the electricity went out. "I hope the lights go out...NOW," David said, snapping his fingers. Nothing happened. He asked if he could have my glow stick, and I said no way. He stared at it on the seat between us, his hand creeping closer, until I snatched it up and stuck it in my shirt.

The hotel manager, a big man with a walkie-talkie, stood in the center of the room. Everyone hushed. "We're asking for volunteers," he said, hands lifted to the sky. "We need to bring mattresses down from the rooms and stack them against these doors."

"Shit just got real," said a guy with a mullet.

I looked at the lobby doors. It was as if we were in a fish tank. Glass stretched from floor to ceiling, and in it I saw us, the guests, looking surprised. As if alive, the glass rattled. Lightning flashed, we disappeared, and outside it was a whole new world. The roots of a tree twitched in the wind. A branch whipped through the air.

We never heard the wind. The workers had turned the lobby music up loud—tinkly underwater music, as if we were in a La Quinta on the lost island of Atlantis. As if we had already sunk.

Matthew volunteered for mattress duty. When he got up to join the rest of the helpers, my heart grew six sizes. He looked manly but calm in his basketball shorts and undershirt. It was how he'd looked in the boxing ring, minus the cigarettes and lighter tucked into his waistband. The crybaby in the shorty-shorts joined the group, and so did a few ladies. Big Gene stayed with us—he has a bad back.

"Why do they want mattresses for the doors?" I asked Mom.

"Think about it."

"I'm too tired. Just tell me."

She hesitated. "So no one gets—" She made a slicing motion across her neck.

I was quiet. That didn't look good. *Was* something bad on its way? We would never know until the moment it arrived. That's the problem with TERRIBLE EVENTS. They never call ahead. "Are we going to get sucked into the sky? Is that glass going to kill us?"

"Opal."

"But you just made the sign—the universal sign for throat-cutting."

"JEAN."

"I'm serious."

Mom sighed and closed her eyes.

"Are you meditating?"

She nodded.

"About the tornado?"

"Mhhmmm."

I call it checking in with her inner Magic 8 Ball. You can ask Mom any question—*Does Lyric like me? Will I get an I-phone for my birthday?*—and she'll come up with the right answer. Last fall I asked, "Will I get my period before Christmas vacation?"

"No, absolutely not," she said. And even though I was mad because why add the "absolutely not" in such a rude way, she was right.

Her chest rose and fell as her breathing slowed. Her arm was warm against mine, and I inhaled her smell of vanilla body spray and sweat. She wore the same faded T-shirt she'd worn on the plane: four cats in KISS makeup, the word HISS underneath.

Just when I thought she'd fallen asleep, she came to. "No," she said, blue eyes bright. "I would be very surprised if anything happened. I believe we will sit here for another half hour, then go up and go to bed." She paused, and when she spoke again, her voice was low. David had fallen asleep, slumped at her side, his light stick opened and glowing in his lap. "And isn't it weird," Mom said, "that you can be scared all the time of nothing and everything at once, and then when something happens that should be scary, like an actual big event, like *this*, you don't feel scared at all. You're just...there...and fine."

I told her I'd emailed Dad.

"Really? What did you say?"

"I said the trip was a disaster, that David almost threw up on the plane when we were waiting to get off in Chicago and no one would move, and I was so mad I hoped he'd throw up on everyone. I said I wasn't going to fly again, so I wouldn't see him again, ever, and if he cared, too bad." I took a breath. "I told him I wasn't going to talk on the phone anymore, either, and that his shirt was WAY too big, and it made me REALLY mad and sad, and I wondered why people did the things they—" I bit the inside of my cheek. Why was I crying? My plan was to never cry about my dad again. It was a whole new world. I wiped my eyes. FAIL.

Mom was quiet for a long time. "So, you broke up with

him," she finally said.

"Yeah, I guess."

I waited for her to laugh at me. Or get mad. A part of me *wanted* her to get angry, to say, "Enough of this nonsense. Your dad is your dad for life whether you like it or not. Email him back and tell him you were joking." But she didn't. She just picked up her phone and went back to playing Candy Crush. "Fucking fudge," she whispered under her breath. "It keeps growing. Goddammit." My mom has worse gamer rage than both my brothers combined. I elbowed her. "MOM. Did you hear what I said?"

She nodded.

"Well?"

She set down her phone. "I think you did what you needed to do. Your dad's a big boy. He can handle it." She hesitated. "Do you think you'll one day change your mind?"

"No," I said.

And that was that.

10

The Story of Specky

W hen I was small, there was a girl in my young-fives class at Angling Road Elementary whose house was destroyed by a tornado. She was from Iowa, and she told us about it during Show & Tell. Mimi was a little ghosty girl, her hair fluffy and white. She said that her family's clothes blew all the way to the outlet mall in Williamsburg, twenty miles east. Her mom, who was there with her, nodded. "I found my kitchen towels right outside the Hanes," she said.

"My house flew away," Mimi told us. "We were in the cellar. The wind sucked our hair straight into the sky." Her mother demonstrated, pulling Mimi's ponytail up from her head like an exclamation point.

"Ouch," Mimi whined. She looked like she might cry. We held our breath. Her mother let go. Mimi continued her story. She told us that her dog had disappeared during the storm, then come back SIX days later! The kids ooohhhhd. Mimi's mom went out into the hallway, then returned with the dog that had blown away, then come back, and now lived in Michigan, the same as all of us. We clapped and cheered.

"Sit on your muffins," the teacher said, so we did. "Tick, tock, lock it up," she warned. So we locked our lips and were quiet. Then we each got a turn to pet Mimi's dog. His name was Specky, and he looked all sorts of crazy-eyed, and his ears were twisted this way and that, but he looked happy, too, happy to visit our young-fives class, to show us the story of him. Specky had blown away. He had come back to his family—all the way from the outlet mall in Williamsburg, twenty miles east. Specky had survived.

Tip #6: No matter how twisted and ear-rattling it is, the story of you is good.

11

I stared at a flower on the couch until my eyes spun like pinwheels.

In real life, nothing happened. It was just like Mom said. We sat there. I watched Matt help drag a mattress across the lobby. Somebody tripped. Somebody cursed. We went back upstairs and got in bed.

I lay on my cot and drifted off thinking of Specky. Was he still alive? Did he remember his time in the sky? Mimi's mom had called him a "Blue Heeler." I was so surprised. There was a blue dog? Was Specky blue? I looked closely. He was blue like a shadow. He was *not* blue like an egg. But he was speckled like an egg. I couldn't wait to get home and tell my mom.

The last thing I remember is David asking Mom why they were called *wisdom* teeth. An instant later, I was floating in the hotel swimming pool. I looked around. Something was wrong. The water was a weird Gatorade green, and it was rising higher and higher, rushing across the tile floor, seeping out beneath the glass doors. It wasn't cold or warm—it just was. It felt like nothing, but good too, as if it were holding me in its arms. I closed my eyes. And when I opened them, there was my dad. He stood near the shallow end, smiling the way he does every time he appears in my dreams.

He wore his prison outfit and flip-flops. The toes of his socks were wet.

A blue dog paddled by. I laughed. Then I remembered the

email I'd sent, and my heart sank. In my dream, I *knew* that sending the email meant I had killed my dad. *I* was the murderer. *I* belonged in prison. I tried to explain, but I was treading water, and when I opened my mouth to speak, I started to choke. "I didn't know the J-Pay would kill you," I said, catching my breath. "I didn't know the workers were assassins. I thought it was an email, like a note on paper. I did what I needed to do. You're a big boy, you can handle it. Only now I see you *can't* because you're dead, and it's my fault."

My dad watched me, a curious look on his face, as if I were speaking Martian. My stomach twisted as I got that the dead don't speak our language, that they no longer have a voice. I started to cry. "Are you dead or alive?" I asked, afraid of the answer.

He didn't say anything.

"Are you dead or alive?"

My dad smiled. He stepped into the pool and waded over to me, his shirt slowly darkening as the water crept up to his shoulders. We sat on the steps of the shallow end. His arm touched mine, and when it did, I knew he wasn't dead. I hadn't killed him with my J-Pay. It was a mistake. Gene Jr., my dad, was alive. I leaned against him, feeling the life in his body flowing into and around me, and I knew that he would be that way, alive, for a long time and maybe even forever. "Dad," I said. He held my hand and we sat that way, in the green water, for a long time, until Matthew blasted his Screamo showering music and I woke up.

12

Dear Macklemore,

It was like waking and drowning at once.

In the morning, we ate Frosted Flakes in the lobby. David put orange juice on his. Matthew drank a Mountain Dew then stood outside and smoked. We could see him, but he didn't look at us. Mom and Marlene talked about menopause. "I spend eighty percent of my energy controlling my moods," Mom said.

"Mood control fail," David whispered.

Big Gene rattled his newspaper. "Grandma was hot and not in a good way. She had me living in a walk-in cooler."

"Oh, I did not."

The breakfast room was deserted. Blobs of sunlight wobbled on the floor, and the ghostly underwater music had been replaced by TLC singing "Waterfalls." It was as if the night before had never happened, and my dream of my dad was what was real. I threw away my cereal box and stuffed three Nutri-Grain bars in my pocket for later. The flowers on the couch rattled in my brain. I shook my head and looked away.

After breakfast, I stood on the curb and watched as Mom and the boys piled into Big Gene's car for the final visit. The sky was blue, and the air smelled cold and clean. Workers were already attacking the uprooted tree with a chainsaw. The plan was that I would stay with Marlene. We would go shopping at Target, then have lunch at the Olive Garden. But as I watched Mom slam the door, and everyone disappeared behind Big Gene's tinted windows, I felt panicky.

Marlene rested her hand on my arm. Her nails were pink,

and her diamond rings—she had about seven—glittered in the sunlight and made me think of snow—sparkling new snow before it turns slushy and gray. Maybe she sensed I was frozen. "Go on," she said. "We can always shop for sundresses tonight."

"I'm just...mad." My throat felt choked.

"Why don't you try?"

"Cry?"

"No, *try*." Marlene's voice was kind, and I bit my cheek hard. "I'll come along, and if you want to leave early, I'll be there to drive you back."

I hesitated. Big Gene's car started to roll down the lane. I saw a bird—stick-legged with big blue wings—in the water and cattails across from the hotel. I looked at it. It flapped away. I took a deep breath and ran after my family.

As we drove to Ionia, through a world of rooftops and mud and flooded streets and trashed trees, the dream kept flowering in my mind. It was like the time I smelled the brain in the bucket in the cadaver lab at Mom's work, only good. For a moment, I felt like I could try to see my dad, to at least say goodbye.

I regretted going the minute we pulled into the parking lot. The prison looked ancient in the sunlight, a gray so old it was no color at all. There were more men in the yard circling the track, some of them in T-shirts, their prison shirts tied around their waists.

We sat in the same room, only this time it was nearly empty. It smelled like microwave popcorn and gym socks. Across from us, a white-haired mom and dad sat beside a man I guessed was their son. He wore aviator glasses, and his bangs were brushed down on his forehead as if her were five and not Big Gene's age. The mom and dad hardly said a word, only stared ahead and looked disappointed. One time, the son said something to the mom, and she got up and brought him back a soda from the vend-ing machine. The man was creepy, and I was glad when his people left and the guard led him away.

Dad wore normal prison clothes, his undershirt white beneath the blue. In this outfit he looked more familiar, more like the dad I remembered—I don't know why. But his shoes were small, black and cheap-looking, and when he told us they were his special visiting shoes, I cried because they were too ugly to be special.

"They're *shoes*," Matthew said. "Be glad you get to see Dad. Who cares about his feet?"

"*I* care. He should have nice shoes. Like…Dr. Larsen."

"Who the hell is Dr. Larsen?" Dad asked.

"He does have fancy shoes," Mom said.

"Is Mommy dating Dr. Larsen?"

David laughed. "He's our dentist. He dresses like a lady and his perfume chokes you."

After Matt told the story of the tornado and the mattresses and the dudes that helped move them, some cool, some pussies, it was my turn to sit by Dad. "Were you scared last night?" he asked.

I shook my head.

"Boy, it was windy here." He finished his coffee, then set the Styrofoam cup on the floor. "You could hear it whistling in the hallway. Like a ghost."

"I'm not afraid of ghosts."

"I don't guess you are." Dad jerked his head at David and Matt, who were busy microwaving chili dogs. "Were the boys scared?"

"Yes," I lied.

"Was Mom?"

"Yes," I lied again.

Silence. I stared at the floor. My flip-flops were dirty, my yellow toenail polish chipped.

"What are you thinking of right now?" Dad asked.

"Specky," I said, just for something to say.

"Specky?"

"Yeah."

"Who or what is Specky?"

I smiled. "He was a dog who came to my class when I

was five. He was in a tornado, but he lived—obviously." I sat up straighter in my chair. "He blew all the way to the outlet malls twenty miles away, but he came back for his people. He—" I quit talking. My ears were on fire. I hadn't meant to sound mad. I stared at my feet, my heart beating in my throat.

Dad was quiet. He touched my arm. "I would come back if I could. You know that, right?"

I shrugged.

"I never left, not really." His voice was hollow, and I was afraid he might cry. "I'm always with you, every minute of the day."

"Like a ghost."

"No."

I gave him a look.

"Well, maybe. But a good ghost—a ghost who cares."

I thought of saying *I don't want a ghost, I want a dad*, but I didn't. I knew it would be mean. Imagine you were a Pug and nobody cared about your doggy-ness, they only wanted you to meow. It was like that.

The boys came back. It was David's turn to sit by Dad. I moved next to Mom and rested my head on her shoulder. I sat quietly, everyone talking around me, the fans spinning in the corners, sunlight puddling on the floor. I pictured the world outside the prison, the sky overhead opening like a big blue hand that had been clenched for a long time.

Toward the end of the visit—because I was tired, or because you can only be scared for so long—I started to feel brave, like I could be where I was. I wrestled the baggie of quarters from David. I got up and went to the vending machine and bought the plainest thing I could find: a cup of beef broth. It tasted like warm dog food water. I drank it anyway. I did NOT get sick.

13

Now I am back in my own HOME, SWEET HOME, and I will **NEVER leave again.** It is after school and dark, rain slamming the skylight, Matthew's stereo blasting hardcore reggae, which is a new thing because he is suddenly in love with a girl/busser from Barbados. I am in Mom's big bed with the laptop, my phone, and a Japanese pear. The blankets smell like dog. Sparkle the guinea pig is walking on my stomach. His feet are pink stars, and his sounds are word bubbles, wobbly and cosmic, like he's come to us from outer space and not the pet store at the mall.

David just walked in wearing his PJs and no shirt, his video game headphones around his neck. "The suitcases are on the front porch," he reported.

"Oh really," I said, sarcastically. "We've only been home a week."

"One of them looks like someone slashed it with a machete." He jumped on the bed and made sock monkey noises until I yelled at Mom to make him stop. David has spent the last twenty-four hours in his room playing video games with some kid from his first grade class who now lives in Buffalo. He got really excited, and Matt and I could hear him yelling all the way down the hall. Last night when Mom was doing laundry, she heard him say, "How do you like that, BITCH," and he got his mouse taken away.

The visit with my dad, the shoes, the fact that *we left him*, still bothers me. At the same time, the dream has stayed with me. I'll be playing my djembe, or swinging on the swings in the rain after school, and it will come back, the feeling of goodness, like a happy frog stuck in the muck of my heart.

My cold blue world is gone.

I am full of something new, something green and hopping and free.

Last night when I was looking at videos of dogs twerking on YouTube, my friend Georgia texted: *OMG, my sis just got us tix to Mklmre. U in?!!*

WHAT??!!

I ran downstairs, tripping over our black Lab Monkeygirl, aka "the whale," who likes to sleep in the kitchen doorway.

Out of breath, I told Mom about the show. I thought she would be excited, but she was all, "no way in hell, you're twelve, you're not going, I don't care how cute the guy is."

WHAT THE MMMPP?!!

I reminded her that she had gone to concerts when she was twelve.

"Yes, I did. The Doobie Brothers. But that was—"

"The Doobie Brothers," Matt laughed, thwacking a spoonful of peanut butter into a mixing bowl.

"—different," Mom continued. "It was the 70s. There weren't that many people on the planet."

"What does the PLANET have to do with it?"

"You're way too overprotective." Matt picked up his giant bowl of cereal, peanut butter, and soy milk and walked out of the kitchen. "You're fear-based," he added, shaking his head. "You live your life in fear."

That's Matt's new thing, that our mom is "fear-based" whenever she won't do what he wants, like drive him across town in rush hour traffic.

Mom sighed. She opened a can of Diet Coke and stared out the kitchen window at the rhododendrons spilling over the fence. During the day they were hot pink. Now, at dusk in the rain, they were gray.

Her friend Richard, who was fixing our Kirby, tried to talk her down. He reminded her that my birthday is in a week, and

I will be thirteen, a teenager, by the day of the show. "Opal is a good girl," he said, pulling a dog-hair-covered sock from the hose. "She has a good head on her shoulders. Let her have some fun." Mom didn't answer, only yelled up the stairs at Matt to quit vacuuming up his socks. But later that night she got online and bought two more tickets—for Matt and one of his friends—the seats five rows behind mine and Georgia's. "A hundred bucks," she said, showing me the confirmation email. "You're going to be doing a LOT of dishes."

So guess what, Macklemore? I will be at your show with my friend Georgia, my big brother/chaperone Matt, and the party-buddy of his choice. You won't see me—we'll be way at the top of the Rose Garden—but I'll be there, a spark of light in the crowd, watching you with a smile on my face and a green green heart.

Love,

Your number one fan, and not in a creeper way like Stan,

Opal Jean <3

Made in the USA
Monee, IL
03 December 2019